Dear Parent:

Your child's love of rea

Every child learns to read in a differe
speed. Some go back and forth betw
favorite books again and again. Othei
order. You can help your young reader improve and become more
confident by encouraging his or her own interests and abilities. From
books your child reads with you to the first books he or she reads
alone, there are I Can Read Books for every stage of reading:

SHARED READING
Basic language, word repetition, and whimsical illustrations,
ideal for sharing with your emergent reader

BEGINNING READING
Short sentences, familiar words, and simple concepts
for children eager to read on their own

READING WITH HELP
Engaging stories, longer sentences, and language play
for developing readers

READING ALONE
Complex plots, challenging vocabulary, and high-interest topics
for the independent reader

I Can Read Books have introduced children to the joy of reading
since 1957. Featuring award-winning authors and illustrators and a
fabulous cast of beloved characters, I Can Read Books set the
standard for beginning readers.

A lifetime of discovery begins with the magical words "I Can Read!"

*Visit www.icanread.com for information
on enriching your child's reading experience.*

For Frank and the stories to come
—R.S.

I Can Read® and I Can Read Book® are trademarks of HarperCollins Publishers.

Splat the Cat and the Cat in the Moon
Copyright © 2020 by Rob Scotton
All rights reserved. Manufactured in U.S.A. No part of this book may be used or reproduced in any manner whatsoever without written permission except in the case of brief quotations embodied in critical articles and reviews. For information address HarperCollins Children's Books, a division of HarperCollins Publishers, 195 Broadway, New York, NY 10007.
www.icanread.com

Library of Congress Control Number: 2019956271
ISBN 978-0-06-269712-7 (trade bdg)—ISBN 978-0-06-269711-0 (pbk.)

20 21 22 23 24 LSCC 10 9 8 7 6 5 4 3 2
❖   First Edition

Splat the Cat

and the Cat in the Moon

Based on the bestselling books by Rob Scotton
Cover art by Rick Farley
Text by Laura Driscoll
Interior illustrations by Robert Eberz

HARPER

An Imprint of HarperCollinsPublishers

Splat and Plank were walking home
one night.
Splat gazed up at the full moon.
"Look! The cat in the moon!"
he said.

Plank frowned.

"That's ridiculous," he said.

"There is no such thing

as a cat in the moon."

Splat pulled out his sketch pad.

He did a quick drawing.

"See his face?" Splat asked.

"Those are craters," Plank said.

"They're big dents
on the moon's surface.

Trust me.

I know all about space."

Plank was a big space fan.

He had shirts

with space jokes on them.

His science poster

always got an A+.

Plank even had glow-in-the-dark stars
on his bedroom ceiling!

SOLAR SYSTEM A+

Neptune

Venus

Jupiter

SUN

Uranus

Mars

Mercury

Earth

Saturn

#1

"I'm basically an expert on space.

Those are definitely craters,"

Plank said.

"Cat face!" Splat yelled.

"Craters!" Plank shouted.

Seymour had his own thoughts
about the moon.
But Splat and Plank
were too busy arguing
to notice Seymour.

"Come on!

I'll show you," said Plank.

Plank led the way

to the shed in his yard.

"Whoa," whispered Splat.

There was a huge telescope

inside the shed.

Splat had never seen one so enormous.

Plank aimed the telescope

at the moon.

He looked through the eyepiece.

"Look at that!" Plank said.

Here is what Plank saw.

Splat looked through the telescope.

Here is what Splat saw.

"Now you see?" Plank asked.

Splat nodded.

"Yep, I see," Splat said.

"The cat in the moon!"

Plank looked again.

"I see craters."

Splat nudged Plank out of the way.

"No way," Splat said,

staring through the telescope.

Seymour pointed to his cheese,
but no one saw him.

"Look again!" Plank said.

"You look again!" Splat said.

Splat and Plank got so loud
they didn't see Seymour slip away.

Then Splat slipped
on an old roller skate.
Whoa!
He flew into the air.
He hit the telescope.

The telescope flew off its stand.

Splat landed on the floor.

The telescope landed on Splat.

Splat!

"Splat, say something!

Are you okay?" asked Plank.

"I caught your telescope,"
said Splat with a big smile.

Together, Splat and Plank

got the telescope back on its stand.

Plank aimed it at the moon again.

Plank looked.

This is what he saw.

Splat looked.

Splat saw the same moon as Plank.

And this is what

they did *not* see.